THE DINOSAUR THAT POOPED A LOT!

Tom Fletcher and Dougie Poynter
Illustrated by Garry Parsons

My
name is

....

and I celebrated WORLD BOOK DAY 2015 with this brilliant gift
from my local Bookseller and RED FOX.

RED FOX

D0434181

Danny and Dinosaur have fun together,
Today they could not — it was terrible weather.
So they both lay there thinking of times they'd had fun,
Because thinking of fun is better than none!
"I loved our adventure in space!" Danny said,
So they closed their eyes tight and went back in their hea

"We're in space!" Danny said, as they floated around,
But the dinosaur's tum made a rumbling sound.

"Is it time to have lunch?" Danny looked at his watch.
      Then he looked all around for the dino's lunchbox.
Danny started to worry, then started to panic . . .
      They'd left their packed lunches back home on their planet!
With no food on board, what did Dinosaur do?
      It munched and it chewed and it nom-nom-nommed too!

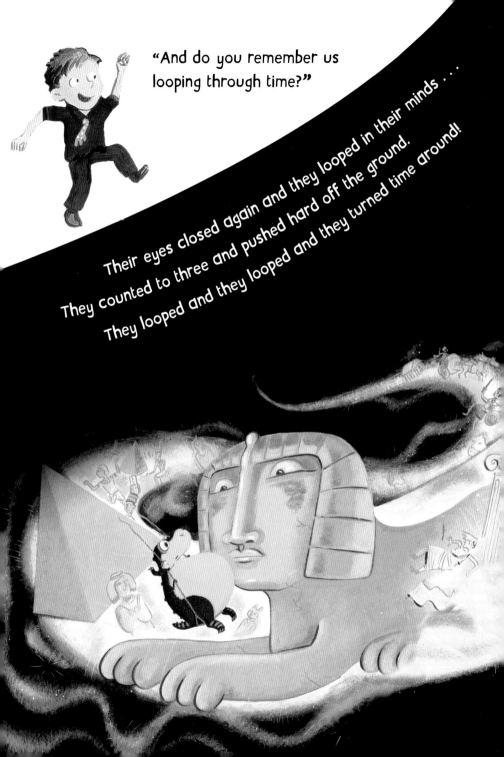

"And do you remember us
looping through time?"

Their eyes closed again and they looped in their minds . . .
They counted to three and pushed hard off the ground.
They looped and they looped and they turned time around!

"We swung back in time, we were trying to play,"
Said Danny to Dino Dudes B, C and A.
But with three extra Dino Dudes joining the group,
It made them too heavy to time-travel loop!

"Dinosaur, I can't remember," Dan said.
"How did we get home? It's just not in my head."

The dinosaur looked deep inside of its mind . . .
    How did they get back home from space and through time?
Danny and Dinosaur thought hard together.
    They thought hard for ages, it felt like for ever!

Then just before Dinosaur quit and gave up,
    Its brain found a memory involving its butt!
Of course, there was only one thing it could do —
    To get them back home, it needed to . . .

POO!

The dinosaur pooped like never before –
Imagine your poo and then times it by four!
It pooped out the space stuff and planets and stars.
It pooped out volcanoes and things from the past.

If you thought that was all, I'm afraid it was not –
When Dinosaur poops, it poops quite a lot!
It pooped them through time, it pooped them through space
It pooped them back home with a smile on its face.

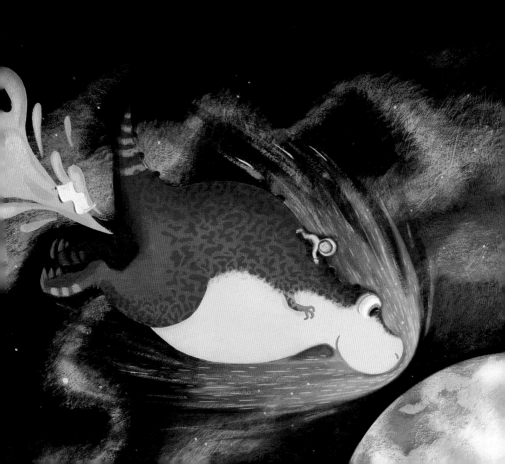

And so Danny laughed, and Dino did too,
Because memories are fun when they're all about poo!

Join Danny and Dinosaur for more adventures:

THE DINOSAUR THAT POOPED A LOT!
A Red Fox Book 978 1 782 95491 0

Published in Great Britain by Red Fox,
an imprint of Random House Children's Publishers UK
A Penguin Random House Company

Penguin
Random House
UK

This edition published 2015
Extracts from *The Dinosaur That Pooped a Planet!* published by Red Fox in 2013
Extracts from *The Dinosaur That Pooped the Past!* published by Red Fox in 2014

1 3 5 7 9 10 8 6 4 2

Text copyright © Tom Fletcher and Dougie Poynter, 2013, 2014, 2015 Illustrations copyright © Random House Children's Publishers UK 2013, 2014, 2015 Illustrations by Garry Parsons The right of Tom Fletcher, Dougie Poynter and Garry Parsons to be identified as the authors and illustrator of this work has been asserted in accordance with the Copyright, Designs and Patents Act 1988. All rights reserved.

Random House Children's Publishers UK, 61–63 Uxbridge Road, London W5 5SA

www.**randomhousechildrens**.co.uk www.**randomhouse**.co.uk

Addresses for companies within The Random House Group Limited can be found at: www.randomhouse.co.uk/offices.htm
THE RANDOM HOUSE GROUP Limited Reg. No. 954009 A CIP catalogue record for this book is available from the British Library.

Printed in China

MIX
Paper from
responsible sources
FSC
www.fsc.org FSC® C020056

Penguin Random House is committed to a sustainable future for our business, our readers and our planet. This book is made from Forest Stewardship Council® certified paper.

This book has been specially written and published for World Book Day 2015. For further information, visit
www.**worldbookday.com.** World Book Day in the UK and Ireland is made possible by generous sponsorship from National Book Tokens, participating publishers, authors, illustrators and booksellers. Booksellers who accept the
£1*World Book Day Book Token bear the full cost of redeeming it.

World Book Day, World Book Night and **Quick Reads** are annual initiatives designed to encourage everyone in the UK and Ireland — whatever your age — to read more and discover the joy of books and reading for pleasure.

World Book Night is a celebration of books and reading for adults and teens on 23 April, which sees book gifting and celebrations in thousands of communities around the country: www.worldbooknight.org

Quick Reads provides brilliant short new books by bestselling authors to engage adults in reading: www.**quickreads.org.uk**

*€1.50 in Ireland

WORLD
BOOK
DAY
5 MARCH 2015

WORLD **BOOK** DAY *fest*

A **BIG**, HAPPY, BOOKY CELEBRATION OF READING

» Want to READ more? «

VISIT your local bookshop

- Get great recommendations for what to read next
- Meet your favourite authors & illustrators at brilliant events
- Discover books you never even knew existed!

 FIND YOUR LOCAL BOOKSHOP **www.booksellers.org.uk/ bookshopsearch**

JOIN your local library

You can browse and borrow from a HUGE selection of books and get recommendations of what to read next from expert librarians—all for **FREE**! You can also discover libraries' wonderful children's and family reading activities.

 FIND YOUR LOCAL LIBRARY **www.findalibrary.co.uk**

Get ONLINE!

 Visit WORLDBOOKDAY.COM to discover a whole new world of books!

- Downloads and activities for **FAB** books and authors
- Cool games, trailers and videos
- Author events in your area
- News, competitions and new books—all in a **FREE** monthly email

 **and MORE!**